P9-CRD-061

First published in the United States, Great Britain, Australia, and New Zealand
in 1994 by North-South Books, an imprint of Nord-Süd Verlag.

Copyright © 1993 by Michael Neugebauer Verlag AG
First published in Switzerland under the title Ich wünscht' ich wär . . . ein Löwe.
by Michael Neugebauer Verlag AG, Gossau Zurich.

Distributed in the United States by North-South Books, Inc., New York.

Library of Congress Cataloging-in-Publication Data is available
A CIP catalogue record for this book is available from The British Library
ISBN 1-55858-342-4 (trade edition)   10 9 8 7 6 5 4 3 2 1
ISBN 1-55858-343-2 (library edition)   10 9 8 7 6 5 4 3 2 1

Printed in Belgium

A Michael Neugebauer Book

NORTH-SOUTH BOOKS / NEW YORK / LONDON

I Wish I Were...
a Lion

By Eve Tharlet

GRROARRR!

I'm going to catch you

and eat you up!

Don't be scared, Arthur. It's all right...
I was just pretending.

I wish I were a fierce lion.
Then I would be the one
making everyone else afraid.

Whenever I felt like having some fun,

I'd roar at my daddy and make him run.

At school

I could do whatever I chose,

Like eat all the snacks,

and pull Walter's nose.

I'd take over the playground—
they'd all run away.

And I'd swing for an hour,
or maybe all day!

But just how much fun
would all that really be,
To play all alone,
with no one but **me**?

Daddy, Daddy, I don't want to be
a fierce lion and play all by myself.

You can still chase me—
if you want to.

Well, you can chase me, too, Arthur.

And if I do roar at you, little one,

it's just because

I love you so much.

GRROARRR!

Look out, Daddy,

I'm going to eat **you** up!

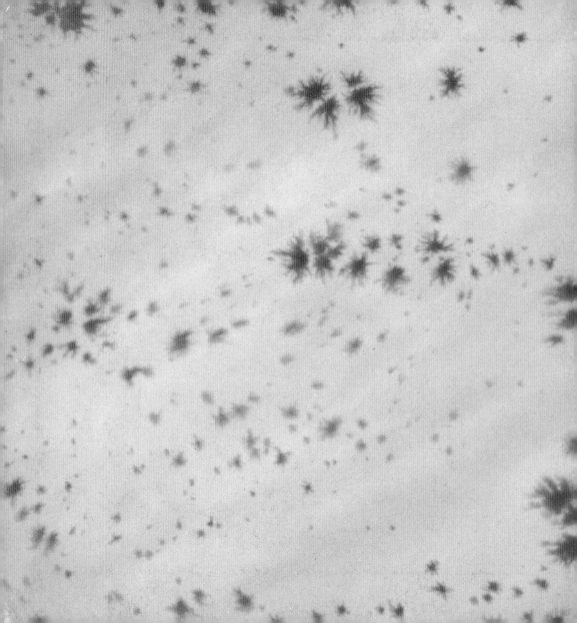